Neath Library
Water Street
Neath Port Talbot Libraries Neath
Llyfrgelloedd Castell-nedd SA11 3EP
Port Talbot 01639 644604

Neath Port Talbot
LIBRARIES
LLYFRGELLOEDD
Castell-nedd Port Talbot
www.npt.gov.uk/libraries

Books should be returned or renewed
by the last date stamped above.
Dylid dychwelyd llyfrau neu en hadnewyddu erbyn
y dyddiad olaf a nodir uchod.

nosy

Granny C was (*whisper it!*) a witch, so sometimes *her* ideas were a tiny bit … different.

"Pumpkin pop!" giggled Pandora's friends. Bluebell, Nellie, Clover and Jake liked Pandora's witchy granny very much.

Once her pet frog had magicked their teacher's clothes away, leaving him in just his underpants!

"Or we could have both?" suggested Pandora as Granny Podmore now looked quite glum.

"Perfect!" cried the grannies and they got to work.

Granny Podmore filled a jug with watery squash while Granny Crow fired up her cauldron and started to toss in ingredients…

"Thirteen tiny pumpkins … ten pints of stuff-and-nonsense … and a good-sized squirt of popping-juice. There!" she smiled.

While the potion brewed, Pandora and
her friends made spooky decorations.
Nellie draped sheets over tables and chairs
to make them look like ghosts, Pandora
made pom-pom spiders from
wool, Clover did pipe-cleaner
snakes, and Bluebell and

Jake turned an old cardboard box into a fantastic spooky castle!

As they worked, Granny Podmore flitted about flicking her duster at anything that got a bit too messy, while humming happy tunes with Granny Crow.

That's better, thought
Pandora. She liked it
when her grannies got
along.

In no time at all Pandora's
plain lounge looked like
a haunted wood. And
Pandora, being a witch
like Granny Crow,
loved it!

"Oh, but I wish
we had glitter," said
Pandora, "to sprinkle
on the castle, like frost."

"Here – I'll do it!"
chirped Granny Crow.
She waved her wand
and pot after pot
of sparkly glitter
appeared.

"Hooray!" cheered the children, grabbing the pots and glittering everything in sight.

"Oh, but the MESS!" gasped Granny Podmore. This called for emergency action!

Scurrying to the cupboard, back she came with her super-sucky hoover. It looked like an octopus with a big smiley face, and its tentacles were tubes with brushes and nozzles on the ends.

"Lucky I brought Ollie!" Granny Podmore nodded. She aimed a tentacle at the floor and…

SUCK!

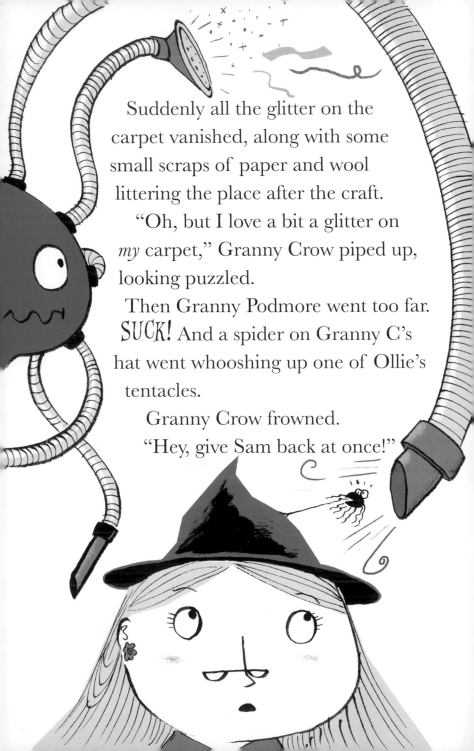

Suddenly all the glitter on the carpet vanished, along with some small scraps of paper and wool littering the place after the craft.

"Oh, but I love a bit a glitter on *my* carpet," Granny Crow piped up, looking puzzled.

Then Granny Podmore went too far. SUCK! And a spider on Granny C's hat went whooshing up one of Ollie's tentacles.

Granny Crow frowned.

"Hey, give Sam back at once!"

When Sam, the pet spider, was back in place, it was time to start on the party food.

Granny Podmore baked her special gingerbread men and made some yummy (and very neat) jam sandwiches. Granny Crow, however, only followed *magical* recipes...

With a flick of her wand, jars and bottles appeared in ALL shapes and sizes. One bottle looked like a crescent moon and was filled with a bright silver powder. The label said Moonshine.

"*Wow,*" gasped Clover, "*real moon!*"

Another star-shaped jar had fluffy balls inside which floated about like dandelion clocks.

"Those are fairy wishes," Granny Crow nodded. "They make your fairy cakes taste of anything you wish for!"

Smiling, she opened her magical cookbook and helped the children with the recipes.

FROM TRUMPING TOAD TRIFLES to SUGAR PLUM MICE: 101 MAGIC RECIPES

With just two *tiny* sprinkles of Moonshine
their blackcurrant jelly turned from purple
to silver and sparkled like the shiniest
moon!

Then everyone whisked up some fairy
cake mixture, putting a fairy wish in every
cake case.

When the cakes were baked, Jake tested one to see if you *really* tasted what you wished for…

"Yep!" he grinned, licking his lips. "Fish and chips!"

When the last tray of biscuits was in the oven, Granny Podmore and Pandora went into the lounge to make some decorations for the party table.

Granny Podmore folded some plain white napkins into the *neatest* swans. Then they made some terrifically tidy paper-chains.

"Let's show the others!" beamed Pandora. But back in the kitchen things weren't quite so spick and span.

Granny C had been making some "little extras" and the place was now splattered in all sorts! Her food might be magical, but boy – what a messy chef!

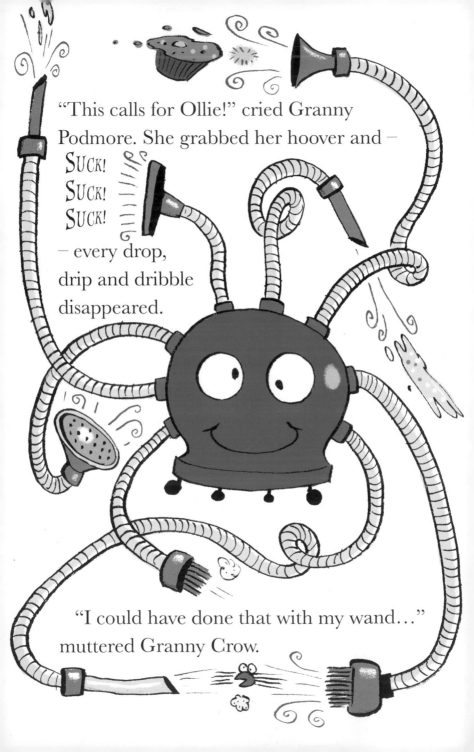

"This calls for Ollie!" cried Granny Podmore. She grabbed her hoover and –

SUCK!
SUCK!
SUCK!

– every drop, drip and dribble disappeared.

"I could have done that with my wand…" muttered Granny Crow.

Now everyone took the
delicious food to the party table.

"Neat swans!" said Bluebell.

"Thank you!" said Granny Podmore.

Granny Crow's food looked wonderful
too. There were bat-shaped biscuits that
hung around the bowls, and a blancmange
cat (that actually meowed!). There were
chocolate roll snail-cakes, broomstick crisps
that really flew, and bright orange Pumpkin
pop now simmered in Granny Crow's
cauldron.

The party was due to start at any minute and lots of friends would be coming.

"Oh, but we haven't got *costumes*!" Pandora gasped.

She and Granny Crow waved their wands together and everyone found themselves dressed up.

Jake was a vampire-bat, Nellie was a witch, Pandora was a spider, Bluebell was a ghost and Clover was a fluffy little werewolf.

"I-I don't need a costume!" Granny Podmore quickly said. Costumes could be so messy.

"Oh, but I have the *perfect* one for you," beamed Granny Crow.

With a flick of her wand, Granny Podmore's plain dress became a magnificent peacock outfit.

"And look!" smiled Granny P, suddenly noticing that the tail was made out of feather dusters. Now she could dust lots of things at the same time!

DING DONG! went the doorbell. It was
party time! Pandora dashed over and
opened the door and an excited crowd
hurried in from the moonlit garden.

There were mummies and monsters.
There were witches and wizards. There
were cats – and bats – and rats!

"Oooh!" gasped everyone when they saw
the place. "*Wicked!*"

Then the
piano started
playing a spooky
tune.

"It's the Fright Night
Party Mix!" Pandora smiled. "My
favourite!"

Granny Crow gathered the children
together. "Take a broomstick each and fly
about," she said, "and when the
music stops catch as many paper
bats as you can!"

Cheering, the children
climbed on to their broomsticks

and zoomed up into the air.

"Yay!" they giggled as
broomsticks bashed and paper
bats zipped about like rockets. And
when stray broom twigs
rained on to the carpet
Granny P was there to

sweep them up
with her tail feathers!

Finally Bluebell won the game
and got a chocolate broomstick
medal. But Granny Crow had *lots*
more magical games up her sleeve.

Next they played Pin-the-Tail-on-the-Werewolf, then Sleeping Lions (though Granny C changed it to *roaring* ones instead!), then Leapfrog with real, live frogs which was fun!

It was all going well. *So* well. Granny Crow was a party sensation! But *then* she went to check on her Pumpkin pop…

"Oh," sighed Granny, peering into the cauldron. "I don't think it's poppy enough."

Pandora looked at her nervously. She really hoped Granny wouldn't spoil things by going too far…

"I think it's fine!" Pandora gulped.

"Ummm … no," said Granny. "It needs more oomph! Just one last *teeny-tiny* spell, that's all."

Pandora had a very bad feeling about this. But before she could stop her, Granny swished her wand and uttered the oomph-iest spell she knew…

"POPPIOCIOUS!"

In a flash of starry light the cauldron started shaking. Then POP went the pop!

Super-fizzy potion now blooped over the sides, and small orange pumpkins were popping out everywhere wearing cheeky little grins on their faces.

"Oh!" Granny Crow jumped in shock *and her wand tumbled into the cauldron!*

"Don't worry!" she spluttered, as a crowd gathered round. "I'm in control!"

But things had never been more OUT of control. The carpet was disappearing under a sticky orange ocean and the pumpkins (wound up on super-fizzy pop) were now having a crazy food-fight.

"I'll see to this!" Granny Podmore nodded.

"No! I can do it!" cried Granny Crow. "Just trust me!"

Chapter Four

Granny Crow fished her drippy wand from the cauldron. "Oh, it *hates* getting wet," she sighed. It was sparking and letting off a low, growly sound like a burp.

But Pandora had other things on her mind. "Granny!" she pointed. "There! Look at the pumpkins!"

The little horrors were now wearing one of the ghost sheets and were tottering about

wailing, "*Whoooo!*"

Problem was, they couldn't see where they were going and were bumping into *everything*…

Crash! The hat stand toppled on to the piano, which made a loud plonk and sent Cobweb, Granny Crow's nervous cat, shooting up a curtain hissing wildly.

"Yikes!" gulped Pandora, peering around for calm, sensible Granny Podmore. But no! Granny P had disappeared – *just when they needed her*!

Now the ghost spun around and started to head for Jake and Bluebell's

38

brilliant castle. The pesky little pumpkins were going to *ruin* it.

"Eeek!" squeaked Pandora. "Nooooo!"

But then – just in the nick of time – Granny Podmore flew past with her super-sucky hoover.

"Ollie to the rescue!" she yelled with pride, and…

SUUUUUCCCKKKKK!

The gloppy orange ocean disappeared at once and all the naughty pumpkins with it.

BA-DOINK! BA-DOINK! BA-DOINK! they went as they bumped along inside Ollie's tentacles, as though they were riding a crazy waterslide!

Plopping into his tummy, they looked *so* mad. The children watched them through a little round window. They were shaking their fists and stomping their little orange feet.

Pandora's eyes widened but Granny Podmore smiled.

"Don't worry," she said. "They're not hurt in the slightest! And we'll set them free – just not in here. Come with me!"

Everyone followed her into the garden. Then Granny Podmore flicked a switch and Ollie hiccupped the pumpkins back out. To be honest he was glad to be shot of them as the stompy little things were giving him indigestion!

Before the pumpkins could sneak back into the house, Pandora showed them her trampoline, which they thought was the best thing ever! Still wild from the pop, they bounced up and down like they had ants in their little orange pants.

"WHOOPEE!"

Back inside, everyone started jumping around to the spooky disco! Pandora hugged her grannies. It was great that they were so different, but so lovely too.

"So, who's for some Pumpkin pop?" beamed Granny Crow. "I think my wand's fixed again!"

Pandora and Granny Podmore laughed.

"Maybe not, Granny," said Pandora. "I think we've had enough excitement for one night!"

And that was one thing both grannies *had* to agree on!

TEDDY
TROUBLE!

Chapter One

"I'm making a polar bear!" Nellie said.

"I'm doing a *grizzly*," grinned Jake.

"A panda!" cried Bluebell.

"A ballet-bear!" smiled Clover.

"The honey-bears look nice," Pandora nodded.

It was Nellie's birthday and her party was at the Fluffy Friends shop in town. At Fluffy Friends you could make your own teddy. You could *even* record a special message to go inside your bear, so when you pressed its tummy it would talk!

Pandora couldn't wait to start making her bear. Although she *did* hope that Granny – who'd come "to help" – wouldn't get too

excited and go too far...

"Oooh!" smiled Granny, looking at the bears in their snazzy little outfits. "Remember that time," she said to Pandora, "I magicked up a bear in the supermarket? And that *darling* little dragon at your school fête when the barbecue wouldn't light?"

Pandora remembered the *dragon* all right.
As well as the burgers, it had barbecued
half the school field!

"Granny," said Pandora nervously, "um
… have you brought your *wand* today?"

"Of course!" beamed Granny. "I take my
wand everywhere, dear!"

Nodding, Pandora then said in a whisper,
"But Granny, no magic is allowed in bear
shops. I think those are the rules."

"Don't worry," tittered Granny. "I'm here to help! And a little *helpful* magic never hurt *anyone*."

With that, she hurried everyone off
to pick out the bits to make their bears.

Nellie's mum and two Fluffy Friends
assistants trailed along behind. The
assistants wore badges with their names on
– Jess and Tom P.

Pandora thought Jess looked really bored and Tom P seemed terrified of Granny. When she asked if they ever made teddy-*werewolves*, Tom was off to "help at the till" like a shot!

Along the back wall was a tall stack of shelves filled with all the things to make the bears. Pandora spied the honey-bear pieces up on the very top shelf. But they looked *way* too high even for the grown-ups to reach.

Jess was now checking the messages on her phone and Tom P was dusting the till. So Pandora asked Nellie's mum if she thought there might be a ladder they could use.

"Oh, but we don't need a *ladder*," beamed Granny. And out came her wand.

"I can do it!"

Chapter Two

Before Pandora could stop her, Granny
wiggled her wand at the shelves.

Problem was, she waved it a bit too
excitedly and everything started flying off –
fluffy teddy pieces and lots of little outfits:
ballet skirts, swimsuits, explorer clothes,
pyjamas! Groaning, Pandora covered her
eyes.

"Oh no…"

Luckily Jess hadn't seen. She'd been far too busy texting. As for Tom P, he was too scared to say a word.

Nellie's mum, however, looked rather annoyed. Pandora's mum, Moonbeam, had warned her all about Granny's "magical meddling".

"*Pssst – Granny,*" hissed Pandora. "*Please put things right!*"

"Um – yes!" blurted Granny, her cheeks going pink.
"Right away!"

With a flick of her wand, everything was tidy and the children were holding what they needed.

"We're ready!" called Pandora, and Jess looked up.

"OK," she said in a bored voice. "Follow me."

She led them to the Fluffing Machine to fill their bears with fluff.

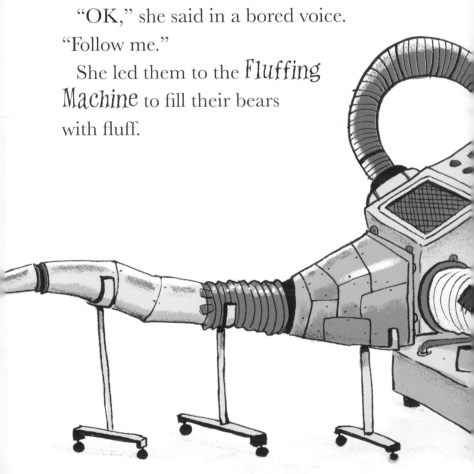

But when she switched it on nothing
happened.

With a sigh, Jess gave the machine a swift
kick. "This is always happening," she said.
The machine whirred to life and some
lights flashed on at once.

"Right," yawned Jess. "Fill your bears
with fluff until they're soft and cuddly."

"Hooray!" cheered the children, getting into a line by the fluff tube.

Nellie went first. Then Jake. Then Clover. Then Bluebell filled Poppy Panda. Finally, it was Pandora's turn.

"Come on, James!" said Pandora brightly, lifting her honey-bear to the fluff tube. But suddenly the machine juddered to a stop. Then fell silent.

"*Ooooohhh,*" groaned Jess, "I'm *sick* of this. Tom P – the machine's stopped *again*. Come over here and give it a boot."

"C-can't!" spluttered Tom, still eyeing Granny nervously. "I've – um – got a bad foot!"

"*Doh…*" puffed Jess, looking *really* fed up. "*Fine…*"

Rolling her eyes, she gave the machine a good, hefty kick. But this time nothing happened. Not a thing.

Jess turned to Pandora who was just behind, still clutching her floppy teddy.

"Silly machine!" tutted Jess. "This time I think it's broken for good."

"Oh no!" squeaked Pandora. Her face fell. All her friends' bears were nice and cuddly!

With that, Granny sidled up. "Don't worry," she whispered, edging out her wand. "You'll soon have a fluffy friend, too!"

"Thanks, Granny," Pandora whispered back. "You're the best!"

Chapter Three

Granny gave her wand a short, sharp flick and the fluffing machine whirred back to life.

"Oh!" said Pandora, trying to sound surprised. Luckily she'd been the only one who'd seen Granny do the spell.

"What's going on?" muttered Jess. The machine sounded healthier than ever.

"Err," said Pandora, quickly filling James

with fluff. "Your kicking must be better than you thought!"

Nellie's mum, however, didn't seem to think so. With narrowed eyes, she looked Granny up and down. But Granny had already slipped her wand away and was whistling innocently.

"Thanks, Granny," said Pandora under her breath, cuddling a beautifully plump James. "But please – *no more magic*! OK?"

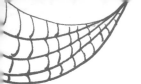

"*Watch me dance!*" squealed Clover's little ballet-bear.

"*Grrrr!*" Jake's grizzly growled.

"*Poppy Panda loves Bluebell!*" Bluebell's panda said brightly.

"*Happy Birthday!*" cried Nellie's polar bear.

And James,
Pandora's honey-
bear, called,
"*Time for tea!*"
The
children
loved
making
their
bears talk and
pressed their tummies *all the time*.

But, after a while, Pandora noticed that something was wrong with James. The more she pressed his tummy, the slower he spoke…

Press!

"Time fooor tea!"

Press!

"Tiiimmee fooooooorrr teeeaa."

Press!

"Tiiiiiiimmmmmmmmmmmeeeeee fooooooooooorrrrrrrrrrrrrrrr teeeeeeaaaaaaaaaaaaaa…"

Upset, Pandora plodded over to Granny and explained that James was broken.

"Oh dear!" said Granny. "Here, let's see."

Taking James, she pressed his tummy gently. But now he wasn't talking at all.

"Don't worry," whispered Granny. "I can sort him out. But I *will* have to use my wand…"

Pandora nodded. It was the only way.

Granny took out her wand and was tapping James's tummy when Nellie skipped over with *her* bear.

Nellie clapped her hands. A talking teddy was the best birthday present ever! But – not only could the two bears *talk* – now it seemed they could *walk* as well!

James jumped to his feet and bounded off. *"Sophie, let's play chase!"*

"Hooray!" cheered Sophie, racing behind. *"Coming!"*

Now *all* the children wanted their bears to "do stuff", and before Nellie's mum could open her mouth, Granny had brought them all to life.

In a blink they were all racing around, which Pandora felt *sure* wasn't allowed.

"*Oh, Granny…*" she said.

"What?" grinned Granny. "They're only having a little bit of fun!"

Jess looked dumbstruck, Tom P looked terrified, and Nellie's mum gasped in horror. Pandora sloped off to join her friends trying to round up the bears. But the teddies were fast. And Poppy Panda was a right little mischief-maker…

Making a bee-line for the machines,
she pressed *all* the buttons, flicked *all* the
switches, and swung on *any* lever she could
reach.

With a rumbly whirr, the machines
sprang to life and started going crazy.

"I don't think they like all their switches flicked at once!" gulped Pandora. The Happy Faces Machine started shooting out bear noses. The Chatterbox Machine began coughing out talk-buttons. And the sewing machines started stitching bear outfits double-quick!

But the Fluffing Machine went the craziest of all. Soon it was burping out great dollops of white fluff.

"*It's snowing!*" Poppy giggled, catching huge pawfuls. Pandora and her friends raced over to Granny.

"Can you round the bears up?" Bluebell puffed. "Of course!" Granny smiled. "Go on, then!" grumbled Nellie's mum. "And while you're at it turn them all back to normal!"

The teddies were now huddled in a corner, whispering. Pandora felt sure they were up to something.

Granny slipped out her wand. But before she could wave it, the bears suddenly broke apart.

Now clutched very tightly in James's fluffy paws was Nellie's mum's basket. Inside it was Nellie's birthday tea. *Uh oh…*

"Hey, come back!" Nellie cried, as the teddies bounded over to the open window and, one by one, flew through it, giggling.

"Really!" spluttered Nellie's mum. "Bare-faced cheek!"

Everyone hurried out into the street but

the teddies had disappeared. Then...

"Look!" cried Pandora, pointing at the pavement. "A clue!"

The teddies had left a trail of fluff – the bits Poppy had collected from the fluffing machine.

"They're playing a 'find-us' game!" squealed Clover.

"Cool!" cried Jake. "Let's follow it!"

The fluff-trail led right down the street, then through a gate into the park. At last, the children found the playful little

bears sitting round a picnic rug, waiting.
On the rug was Nellie's party food, all
laid out just right.

"*Surprise,*" giggled James.

"*A teddy bears' picnic!*"

Their teacher tapped the
bus driver, who
whispered something back.

"Oh no!" cried Mr Bibble. "Not a
puncture!"

All along the bus children started to
chatter.

"Quiet!" Mrs Appleton snapped.

Mrs Appleton was the Year 6 teacher. But on Tuesday afternoons Mr Grimly took her class so that she could help with swimming.

Nobody liked Mrs Appleton. She was as round and sour as a crab apple.

So her nickname was Crabby-Appleton. Crabby for short.

Down Crabby thumped from the back of the bus. But halfway along she stopped.

Granny, who had also come to help, suddenly put up her hand.

"Yes?" barked Crabby.

"Well," Granny smiled, "I'm a whizz at fixing punctures, you know." She whisked out her wand but Crabby glowered.

"Absolutely not!"

Nose in the air, Crabby marched to Mr Bibble. "Well, don't just *sit* there," she scowled. "Come and help me fix that puncture!"

She rounded on the bus driver. "Go and get your tools!"

"But I d-don't have any tools with me," he muttered.

"What?" yelled Crabby sourly. "How ridiculous!"

With that, Granny swept past, her wand held high in the air.

"Eeek!" gulped Pandora. This didn't look good. If Granny did magic after Crabby had said *not* to there was going to be BIG trouble.

And sure enough…

"Look here," smiled Granny, striding off the bus. "I'll just do a *teeny-weeny* spell to change this bus into something that won't get a puncture!"

The children's noses were now pressed to the windows. What would Granny change the bus into?

Crabby marched out, blowing her whistle, but Granny had already waved her wand, and…

When the magic mist cleared, the bus had
gone and five old-fashioned circus caravans
stood there in its place.

Each one was pulled by a big, friendly horse and held six delighted children. Granny had magicked up jugglers too. And acrobats.

"There!" beamed Granny, as Crabby stood gaping. "*Horses* don't get punctures, do they? Hop in!"

Chapter Two

Crowds of people waved from the pavements as the circus headed to the pool. When they got there, Mr Bibble hurried everyone inside.

"And no more nonsense from *you*," sniffed Crabby, as Granny held open the door.

"Nonsense, dear?" said Granny, surprised. She'd saved the day!

Mr Bibble took the boys to get changed

POP!

Now the messy changing room became
the poshest bathroom ever! The showers
had gold taps in the shape of fish, the
floor was made of marble, and a crystal
chandelier twinkled overhead.

"*Wow*," gasped the girls. It looked just like
a palace!

Everyone skipped away to the showers to wash in rainbow bubbles. Pandora, though, stayed by Granny. For Crabby looked crosser than ever and was heading their way…

"How many times," Crabby glowered at Granny, "must I tell you not to meddle! Now I'm warning you – no more *you-know-what*!"

"You know … what?" said Granny, puzzled.

"*Magic*," whispered Pandora.

Before Crabby could utter another cross word, Pandora pointed out it was time for the lesson.

"Right then, girls," called Crabby, "off we go!"

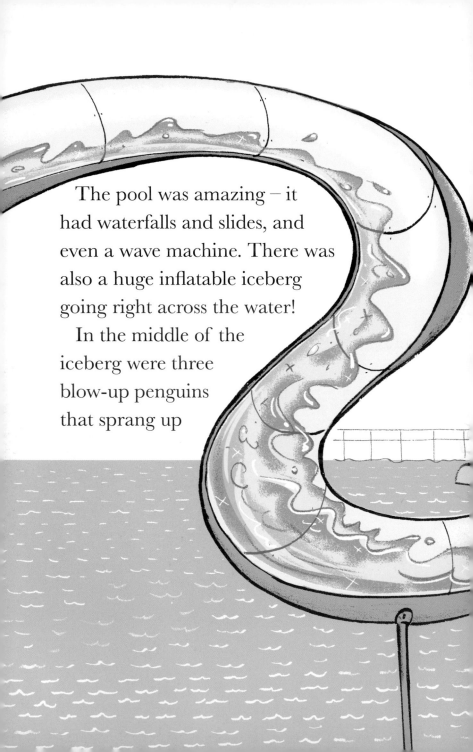

The pool was amazing – it
had waterfalls and slides, and
even a wave machine. There was
also a huge inflatable iceberg
going right across the water!

In the middle of the
iceberg were three
blow-up penguins
that sprang up

and down when you climbed on them.
Pandora's friend, Jake, had had his
swimming party
here, and it had
been really fun!

But today the iceberg and slides were roped off. The waterfalls were turned off too.

"Shame," sighed Pandora.

"Yeah." Nellie nodded.

All they were allowed to do in school lessons was swim back and forth with floats. And Pandora's group was taught by Crabby, who stood on the side the whole time, yelling…

"Kick harder!"

As the children swam *endlessly* from side to side, Granny had to sit sensibly and be "in

charge" of the floats.

But the floats didn't *need* being "in charge" of. Why *would* they? Floats never did anything! So Granny just wriggled, and jiggled, and sighed, and checked the clock as the time ticked on slowly. *Yawn*…

And then, just before the end of the lesson – as Granny sat twiddling her thumbs – she had the most wonderful idea.

Checking to see if the coast was clear, she secretly slipped out her wand. It was time to liven things up a bit, *Granny style*!

Chapter
Three

"Miss!" Jake suddenly yelled from the water. "That penguin over there just winked!"

He pointed at the inflatable.

"Nonsense!" snapped Crabby.

"But Miss – it did!" cried Jake. "I *really* saw it!"

Pandora, who was swimming near the inflatable, looked up *as the penguin winked again*!

"*Uh oh…*" she muttered under her breath. This had to be Granny. It *had* to!

While Crabby and Jake argued on, Pandora swam over to Granny.

"Psst, Granny," she whispered up from the water, "did *you* make that penguin wink?"

"I … *might* have," grinned Granny. "OK

– I did! I just wanted the last five minutes of your lesson to be fun!"

With that, she flicked her wand again and all three penguins started waddling along their iceberg.

"The penguins! Look – they're moving!" Bluebell squealed.

One by one, the penguins plopped into the water where Mr Bibble was blowing

bubbles with his beginners.

"Arrgh!" he spluttered. "W-what's going on?" But Crabby knew all right.

"Pandora's granny!" She nodded crossly. "That's what!"

As Crabby stomped over to Granny, the penguins in the pool were having great fun. The more Mr Bibble shooed them away, the more they jumped on and off their iceberg, sending fountains of water everywhere.

"Stop them!" Mr Bibble called.

"Oh, don't you worry," Crabby puffed. "I will!"

As soon as she was close enough, Crabby snatched the wand from Granny's hand.

"Hey," frowned Granny. "I'll have you know, wands need handling with care."

"And I'll have *you* know," Crabby frowned back, "that magic is not allowed in school swimming lessons!"

Crabby whisked the wand out of arm's reach. But as she did, a swirl of stars came shooting out of it.

"Oh, *now* look what you've done," groaned Granny.

"What?" Crabby glowered.

"You've just gone and cast a *spell*," sighed Granny.

Pandora watched the magical stars as they zipped and zoomed through the air. They sparkled like moonshine and looked brimful of mischief!

A swirl of them swept round the waterfall and it gushed to life at once.

Other stars bounced off a long, straight slide, which turned into a giant rollercoaster. The inflatable iceberg got zapped by stars too and magically grew into a *real* block of shimmering ice!

"Hooray!" cheered the children, splashing off to have fun.

"To the *rollercoaster*!" Nellie called.

But Pandora had spotted a bunch of cheeky stars bouncing up and down on the diving board. They were getting *wilder* by the second. What next?!

Chapter Four

WHOOSH!

The stars dive-bombed into the water and pinged off the wave machine like hailstones.

With a small spurt of bubbles, it blooped to life. Then soft, gentle waves began rippling through the pool.

"Yippee!" cheered the children. Waves were great! Shame Mr Bibble didn't think so.

"Out of the water please, children!" he called.

"Oh, but it's fun!" Bluebell cried. Everyone agreed. No *way* were they getting out now!

Soon children were whizzing down the rollercoaster-slide, playing pirates under the waterfalls and bobbing about in the soft, bouncy waves like dolphins! Up on the iceberg Jake, Clover and Bluebell had just started a game of arctic explorers when Nellie and Pandora appeared.

"This is our flag!" Nellie announced, sticking a float into the ice. Then Pandora declared the new kingdom as their land.

"But

we got here *first*," Bluebell frowned.

"Ah, but you need a *flag* to make it *yours*!" Nellie nodded.

Meanwhile, at the side of the pool, the grown-ups were arguing too. Suddenly, Granny made a grab for her wand but Crabby had seen that coming.

"Oh-no-you-don't!" Crabby puffed, dodging out of the way. But the floor was wet and her foot slipped.

"Help!" shrieked Crabby. "I'm falling!"

Crabby grabbed Granny's arm to steady herself but *Granny* started wobbling too. Then down they both tumbled into the water...

Splash!

"Granny!" gasped Pandora, now swimming towards them. She could see that Crabby still had the wand.

But that's not *all* she could see...

"Giant wave!" yelled Pandora. "Everyone on to the iceberg!"

Squeals of excitement filled the air as children clambered on to the iceberg, along with three penguins, two drippy teachers, and Granny!

A few moments later the massive wave hit with one great foamy CRASH!

"Hey – it's giving us a *ride*," grinned Jake, as the wave nosed their iceberg out of the pool … then out of the door …

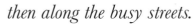

then along the busy streets.

"Beep beep!" cried Pandora, as traffic swerved out of the way.

At last, the iceberg slid to a stop in the middle of Pandora's school playground. It had brought them *all* the way back – and what a ride!

Jumping off, the children started skipping around it.

"Hooray for our ice-bus!" they cried.

Granny got off next, followed by Crabby. Her face was a sea-sicky shade of green and she *still* held Granny's wand.

"Thank *you!*" said Granny, whisking it back into her pocket.

Finally, Mr Bibble staggered from the iceberg. The very last to leave.

Or *was* he…?

"Look!" beamed Pandora, as three little penguins came waddling off behind him.

"New school pets! Yippee!" cheered the children.

Granny looked very pleased too. Fishing in her pocket again, she took out her wand!

"Time to make the school pond just a tiny bit bigger..."

The End